Zombie Soup

by Gina Preston
Illustrated by Mike Corrick

West Exeter

Zombie Soup. Text copyright © 2006, 2017, 2018, 2020 by Gina Preston. Illustrations copyright © 2018, 2019, 2020 by Gina Preston.

This book or parts thereof may not be reproduced in any form, stored in any retrieval system, or transmitted in any form by any means-electronic, mechanical, photocopy, recording, or otherwise-without prior written permission of the publisher, except as provided by United States of America copyright law.

Cover and illustrations by Mike Corrick.

For permission requests write to:
West Exeter Publishing PO Box 7882 Columbus, GA 31908

All Rights Reserved.
ISBN 978-1-7345136-1-5

Library of Congress Control Number: 2020915653
Manufactured in the U.S.A.

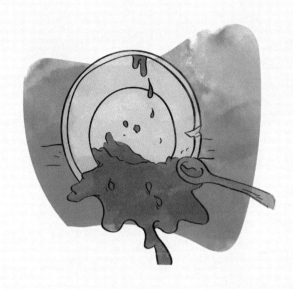

To Seth, my absolute joy and the inspiration for Ben
To Mom and Dad, thank you for the gift of unconditional love
-G.P.

To all my friends and family who have encouraged me along the way
To all the loyal pups that inspired Skippy
-M.C.

"Eat your soup," said Mom.
"I can't," said Ben. "There's a
zombie in my soup."
"Don't be silly," laughed Mom.
"There isn't a zombie in your
soup."

Ben stuck the spoon in his soup and **swished it around**.

"Eww, **red zombie guts**," said Ben.
"Those are not zombie's guts," said Mom.
"That's tomato broth."

"What about these **creepy black eyes** staring at me?" asked Ben. "Those are peas," replied Mom.

GLUNK! went the soup.
"Gross! Green zombie fingers!" gasped Ben.

"It's just broccoli," sighed Mom.

The soup noise
woke up Skippy.
"I'll be right back," said Mom.
"**Eat all your soup**
before you go outside."

When Mom left, Ben smacked his soup.

SPLASH! GLUNK!

The green fingers disappeared.

"Yay! **I did it!**" said Ben.
"No more zombie soup!"
But Skippy wasn't so
sure.

"Arf!" barked Skippy
when he saw

something move.

Ben leaned over the
bowl to get a better
look.

The soup started to bubble, and the bowl began to **rumble**.

"The zombie's **climbing out** of the soup!" cried Ben.

"Hide, Skippy!"
said Ben, and he
dived under
the table.

Skippy **jumped off** the chair and followed Ben.

The **zombie crawled** around on the table above them.

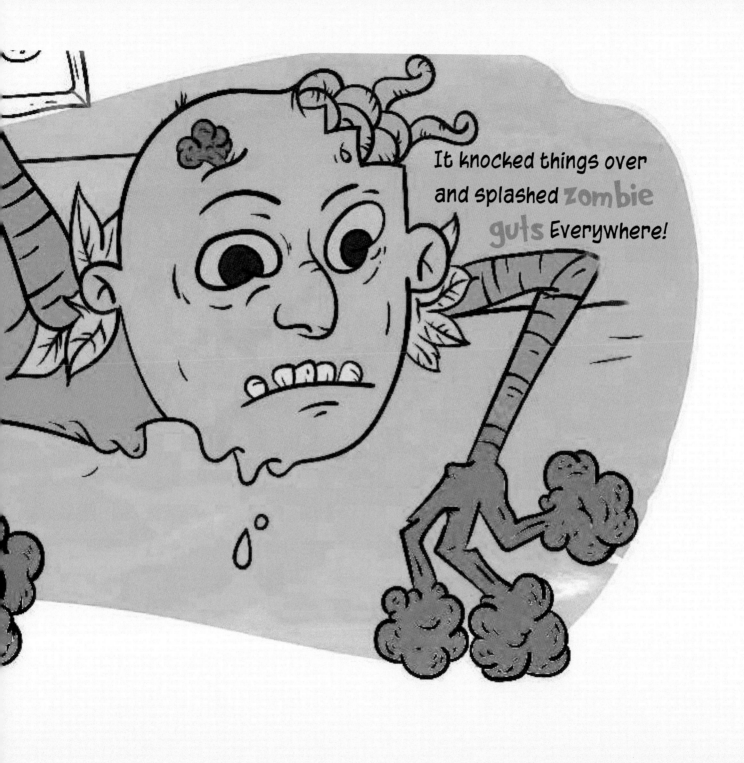

The zombie dropped its **orange arm** over the edge of the table.

It **wriggled its green fingers** looking for Ben.

"Skippy," whispered Ben. "There's a **zombie in our kitchen.**"

"Yip," whimpered Skippy.

Suddenly,
the zombie
**peeked
over** the edge
of the table
and found Ben.

"AHH!" yelled Ben.
Ben and Skippy ran out from under the table.

"**BLARG!**" growled the zombie and came after Ben.

Ben threw his soccer ball at the zombie, but the zombie did not stop.

Ben threw Skippy's rubber bone at the zombie, but the zombie did not stop!

Ben tried to run out of the
kitchen, but it was
too late!

The zombie grabbed Ben
with its arms and
snarled.

"Help!" cried Ben.

"**Woof! Woof!**"
barked Skippy, and he came to the rescue.

Skippy jumped on top of the zombie's head took a huge bite and

SLURRP!

"You did it, Skippy!"
cried Ben.

"No more
zombie
soup!"

Just then, Mom walked in. "I'm glad the **zombie soup** is all gone." she teased. "Now you can go out and play."

"Thanks!" said Ben.

"You're welcome!" said Mom.